Fragile Hearts

A Secret Baby Romance

Spicy & Sweet Insta Love Shorts

R Sullins

www.rsullins.com

rsullinsauthor@gmail.com

Please note: This story was previously published in the anthology Santa Baby 2023

CHARACTER COVER by - Artscandare Book Cover Design

INTRODUCTION

Holly

When my dad, and boss, announced I'd be interviewing Trent Frost, I wasn't sure how I could pull it off. Trent was the hottest hockey player both on and off the ice. He was also notorious for his staunch refusal to allow any journalist near him. But my dad made it very clear my future in the company which had been in our family for generations was on the line.

Trent

I had no intentions on ever breaking the rule I had for reporters. To me, they were some of the worst humans on the planet. But one look at the beautiful woman, was enough to break me. I'd never wanted anything as much as I wanted her. I knew once I had her I would never be the same again.

We just hadn't realized how our one amazing night together would ruin us both.

ONE

HOLLY

I wrung my hands together in my lap out of view of my father as I stared down at the notepad in front of me. I could feel my cheeks burning as the snickers of the men around the conference table that weren't quite muffled reached me. I was quite sure they had intended for them to.

"Dad, are you sure... "

A heavy hand landed flat on the surface at the head of the long mahogany table. "Holly!"

I knew that was code for *shut the fuck up and do what you're told*. So I shut up, though I wasn't happy about it.

My whole life had been planned out since conception. Well, prior to that, if I considered that I was a do-over for my sister. Her life had been planned, but she'd had a backbone and a voice. Her voice was loud and clear when she'd told our parents in no uncertain terms that she wasn't going to be their puppet.

That was twenty years ago. Now, she is happy living far away in a different state, and I am a nineteen-year-old who is still living with her parents.

Why?

Because they learned from what they considered their first mistake.

Everything they considered they did wrong with my sister, Helen, they did the opposite with me. I also suspect they took some psychology classes or something that taught them how to be manipulative assholes.

I knew they were manipulating me, molding me to be their "perfect" offspring, and it twisted me inside. Unfortunately, it still worked. I was well and truly manipulated, even if I often wished I had the same courage my sister had.

"Say the word, Holly Berry, I will have you on the first plane to me. You're an adult now. They can't do shit to me."

Helen had been trying to set me free for years. Honestly, I was surprised that our parents had allowed us to have a relationship at all.

"Holly, my office."

All around me, chairs were being scraped against the floor as people stood and made their way out of the conference room and headed to their desks to get started on whatever they had been assigned by my dad, the big boss and owner of one of the most prestigious online news sites in the country.

And I was supposed to be his heir. It didn't matter that I had no desire to go into journalism, run a business, or prove myself worthy to men who had been working for the company for longer than I had been alive and expected the job I was being handed just because of my last name.

I meekly stood up, ignoring the mocking, pitying looks of the last of those to leave, and glanced out of the window instead. The sky was gray. Large, puffy dark clouds slowly inched along as they threatened to dump more snow on the city. I wished they would.

Fresh snow always made things feel fresh and new again. At least for a little while.

I turned away from the window and reluctantly walked down the long hallway, past the stares and laughter, the whispered "daddy's girl" I hated so much. If they only knew I wanted nothing to do with this kind of nepotism.

I stood just inside the open doorway and waited for my dad to acknowledge me. He was on the phone, barking an order into it, but it didn't sound overly important. If it were, the door would have been closed, and his face would have been red.

The phone crashed into the cradle, making me jump from my contemplation of the puffy clouds again, and I clutched the notebook tighter to my chest as I swung my head to face my father.

"Door!" He barked out and jerked his chin toward one of the chairs in front of the desk.

With an internal sigh, I softly closed the door and sat down, nervously crossing my ankles and smoothing my long skirt. I was probably going to get another lecture about the history of the company and the importance of legacy. About how it was my responsibility to keep what my great-grandfather had started all those years ago thriving and moving into the next great age of our future. I hadn't expected the ultimatum.

I set the notepad in my lap and took my pen in hand, ready to take notes if he required me to.

"Holly," he paused, let out a great big sigh, and pinched the bridge of his nose. It was the first time I ever noticed his age, ever noticed that my dad was actually getting old. When he looked back up at me, his face seemed even more lined than usual, and there were deep circles around his eyes. But inside his gaze, he seemed more determined than I had ever seen him. An icy fingernail of foreboding scraped up my spine.

"Trent Frost is the top NHL player in the country right now. No other news organization has been able to get an interview with him since he came on the scene ten years ago. He is hot enough to melt the ice he skates on and scores enough on and off the ice to break records and make nuns blush."

I sat, staring wide-eyed at my father. When he had announced I'd be interviewing Trent Frost in the conference room, there had been a small eruption of smothered laughter that the men had done their best to end quickly before the boss could glare them to death. I had sat frozen for a long moment, not entirely under-standing why my father would assign me anything.

I was still in the watch-and-learn phase. I was headed to school in the spring after a short break during which my parents had thought it would be best for me to learn what this whole future thing was all about. I honestly couldn't imagine what he could possibly be thinking right now.

"You are the future of this company. As such, it is you who needs to prove your loyalty and commitment. I expect you to do whatever it takes to get an interview from this man." I had been given direct orders my whole life and knew when my father fully expected to be obeyed. There were times when it was okay to ques-tion him. This was not one of those times. And yet, the look in his gaze and the implication I read in the tone of his voice had me wanting to question everything. "Don't let me down."

I swallowed and did the one thing I was taught to do. I nodded, said, "Yes, Dad," and went to my little office I hadn't earned on merit, but had gained me plenty of hate-filled glares, to start making phone calls until I could schedule an interview with one Mr. Trent Frost.

Two

Holly

I smiled, sure it looked more like a grimace, at the other reporters that stood in a cluster near me. The hallway was much warmer than it had been down near the ice, and I was starting to sweat inside my heavy jacket. I hastily glanced back down at the new notebook I bought just for this interview when it looked like one of the men appeared to actually start to say something to me.

I dug through my messenger bag, for what, I had no idea. I just needed to appear busy. I couldn't let on that these men intimidated me. Though considering they were reporters, I was pretty sure they already knew.

"What's your article about?" The friendly voice jerked me from my pretend search. He continued without waiting for a response as he leaned casually against the wall next to me, likely trying to appear sophisticated. I had to hold back the eye roll. His obviousness was something I had seen every single day since my dad started taking me to the office. "I've got a one-on-one with the team captain. He only gives out interviews a few times a year." He tossed a smile my way, gauging if I was offering the appropriate amount of impressed. Instead, I was studying the garland that was drooping from the ceiling. I had almost forgotten it was going to be Christmas in just a couple of days. We didn't really celebrate Christmas in our family. The business took precedence over that part of our lives, too.

A throat clearing jerked me from the thought of the sad ham dinner we would have with the beautiful holiday display in the center of the table and the one gift that my parents would slide across the table to me. I already knew it would be a new Cartier watch. Every year, I received the same one. I didn't know if they forgot or if they thought I needed an updated one. I never asked.

"I'm sorry, what?" I glanced over to the blond in his blue polo and tan slacks and tilted my head, wondering if he had said something else.

He straightened up and ran a hand over the side of his head. It was so odd to see that not a single strand of his hair moved. "I asked if you'd like to have a cup of coffee after this?" He tried out his smile again, and I blinked at the bright whiteness of his teeth. That didn't look natural. "I could help you with your article." He leaned in a little more, and I got a strong whiff of his expensive cologne. It was the same one my dad used, making me need to cover my mouth to conceal the gag I couldn't hold back. "You know, I am really making a name for myself at my news company. I could put in a good word for you if we click. Maybe get you a good job or... "

"Miss Fields?" A voice called from down the hall, and I spun around quickly, almost losing my balance on the high heels I hadn't wanted to wear, but my dad insisted would make me look more approachable. Approachable, right.

"Thank god. I mean... yes?" I cleared my throat and took

several steps away from the reporter, who obviously didn't know how to read a person as well as he should have been able to.

There was a tall, thin man who looked frazzled, holding a clipboard and hurrying toward me. He didn't look very happy. If anything, I'd say he looked rather upset. He was wearing a light pink button-down shirt with a dark gray tie and matching slacks. His brown hair was styled in a pompadour, and I could easily see him as someone who would be fun to hang around with. If he weren't frowning at me.

As he approached, I saw the double doors of the locker room open up, and the noise immediately grew in volume as the hockey players began to emerge. They were large and intimidating, but I didn't get to see much more of them than I had while watching them on the ice since the other journalists began to swarm them immediately. I had no idea which one was my guy. I mean, the guy I was supposed to be having an interview with.

I looked down at my watch and saw that my appointment was supposed to be in five minutes. I had been instructed to wait in the hallway with the rest of the reporters, and someone would be along to collect me.

I lifted my hand to offer the man with the clipboard a greeting and a smile. "Hello, I'm Holly Fields. You're Fred Pine?"

His smile was friendly, but I could tell he was forcing it. A ball of dread started to fill my stomach. I didn't know what Dad would do if I couldn't pull off this interview, but I was sure I didn't want to find out.

"Yes, I spoke to you on the phone." He sighed and looked down at his clipboard before bringing his apologetic gaze back up to meet mine. He started to speak but paused, looking around at those near us, causing me to notice that the overly friendly guy from before was still watching pretty closely. I thought he would have been busy interviewing like the other journalists. Fred took me lightly by the arm and pulled me a few feet away before lowering his voice.

"Look, I have to be completely honest with you. I just started as Mr. Frost's assistant a few days ago. We hadn't gone over much of his... preferences until, well, just now. Basically, I had no idea that he doesn't do interviews. Ever." He grimaced. "I'm really sorry for wasting your time, Miss Fields. I take complete responsibility for this unfortunate situation."

I could tell how uncomfortable he was and felt for him. I bit the inside of my cheek to hold back the flood of emotions at what this failure would mean for me. I straightened my shoulders back and gave Fred my brightest smile, placing my hand on his arm. "Please, it's okay. I can see how bad you feel. It's really okay. No harm done. If anything ever changes, please feel free to give me a call, though, okay?"

He nearly sagged with relief, making me know I had done the right thing. There was no sense in two of us being upset over this. "Thank you, Miss Fields. I will absolutely call you if anything changes." His smile was genuine and sweet. I had to blink quickly to hold back another rush of emotions. It was so rare to be smiled at that way.

I nodded and was about to turn to walk away, my mind already whirling with how I was going to explain this to my dad, when both of us gave startled jumps at a barked, "Fred!" coming from down the hall.

We both turned at the same time to look at a tall man walking briskly toward us. He was passing the group of people all speaking loudly over each other, questions being thrown around, and the occasional raucous laughter. As soon as I saw him, my breath caught in my throat.

He was as tall and broad as most of the other players, his athletic build easily setting him apart from the group of journalists. He was so much more intense than anyone else, though. His eyes were what held most of the intensity, though his muscles seemed to be rigid under his tight black t-shirt and blue jeans. He was also the most handsome man I had ever seen.

His square jaw was tight as if he were grinding his teeth, and his dark blue eyes looked angry, zeroed in on where my hand was still resting on Fred's arm. I immediately snatched it back, clenching my fingers into a fist and digging my blunt nails into my palm. What I really wanted to do was run my fingertips over the crease between his straight, dark brown eyebrows. At the removal of my hand, he seemed to relax just the tiniest fraction.

Fred stepped forward toward the angry man. "Mr. Frost, I was coming back to you. I was just explaining the situation to Miss Fields and giving her my apologies for wasting her time."

The man's eyes hadn't left mine since Fred began to speak, and I found myself needing to work harder than usual to keep my composure impassive. I could feel my breathing picking up, regardless of my self-control.

"I've changed my mind." Trent Frost, the hockey player extraordinaire, the man that never does interviews, and the one my dad had insisted I get a story on, stepped past a gaping Fred and held out his hand for mine.

I slowly unclenched my fist, flexing my fingers. Then, I almost reluctantly held my hand out. As eager as I was to touch this man, I was uncertain if I could handle whatever was promised behind his eyes. When our hands touched, it started as a simple slide of palm against palm, his rough calluses rasping against the softness of my skin. But it was enough to have a tingle run up my back, ending with the hair on the back of my neck standing up. It was as if an electric current had zapped me. My fingers twitched, ready to pull away, but I held steady, not wanting to appear weak.

As he gripped my fingers in a gentle yet firm hold, I felt him stroke his thumb over the top of my hand once, then twice, and I had the ridiculous impression he was trying to wipe the feel of the other man off of my skin and replace it with his. Looking into his eyes, I wasn't sure it was quite so ridiculous after all.

THREE

TRENT

I had been about to fire my newest assistant, or go back and re-fire my previous assistant for not thoroughly preparing their replacement with all that was expected of them. At least my battleax of a publicist understood. I didn't do interviews. Ever. It was in my contract, something I had demanded when I was first signed, and made sure to keep in every newly updated contract since.

I had one reason only for my lack of interest in interviews. I quite simply abhorred journalists. They were nothing but blood-thirsty vultures that would sell their own soul to the devil for an article. I wanted nothing to do with them. So I couldn't explain why I was now holding the hand of one and staring into her eyes as if I were trying to promise her my entire signing bonus if she would just have dinner with me.

She was taller than most women, though her fingers felt small, as if I could easily crush them if I tightened my hold. Her dark brown hair was slick and shiny under the fluorescent lights of the stadium hallway. Her rounded cheeks were flushed, and her pillowy lips parted as she took shallow breaths. The hazel eyes that seemed to have more gold than brown were a mix of scared and excited. I wanted to ask what she was afraid of and fix it for her. I wanted to fix everything for her.

Fred speaking broke into the trance that she had put me in the second I stepped out into the hall, ready to head straight for the parking lot, when I caught sight of my new assistant in a conversation with the most beautiful woman I had ever seen. Seeing her up close, I could tell she wasn't nearly as old as I had thought, though. There was no way this woman was old enough to be a journalist. Not unless she had gone straight to work from high school, skipping college altogether. By the end of the night, I would learn all I needed to.

"Are you sure, Mr. Frost? You were quite clear in the locker room about your policy regarding interviews." I didn't bother sparing Fred a look. I would make sure he got a raise in the morning to compensate for my rudeness tonight, though. After all, his fuck up led to my girl being here in front of me.

"I'm sure, Fred. You can have the rest of the night off. Me and Miss... "

"Holly Fields," she spoke softly, and hearing her voice had my hand tightening on hers before remembering how fragile she felt in my huge hands.

"Beautiful name," I murmured. "We can have the interview at my penthouse. It will be much quieter and less distracting."

Her cheeks bloomed with more color, and I wanted to see for myself how far down that blush went. "Uh, sure. That sounds good." I felt a slight tug on the hand I was holding and reluctantly released my hold, promising myself I would get my hands on her again soon. "I can follow you, or if you'd like, you could give me your address?"

"I can drive you." Then, I would have her at my mercy with a harder chance for her to escape.

She looked around, and I followed her gaze, wondering if she had come with someone that I would need to get rid of. The only person I saw paying close attention to us was some slicked-back douche. The typical asshole journalist that would leave his wife and children at the first chance to make it big with his next story.

I glared a hole through his polo until he finally took his eyes off my girl and met my gaze. He proved to be slightly more intelligent than I had initially taken him for when he swallowed hard, his Adam's apple bobbing in his throat. Then, my opinion immediately lowered again when his eyes darted back over to Holly.

"A friend of yours?" I could hear the venom in my voice. Ask me if I gave a fuck.

"What?" She looked confused and turned her attention to where I was still glaring the asshole down, daring him to make a move. "Him? No, I don't know him."

I grunted. "Good." Finally turning away from the guy who was no obstacle to the girl that was already mine. "Ready for that interview?" I held out my hand for her to take.

There were a few mutters of disbelief behind us at my question, proving that we had an audience after all. Everyone knew my rule, so it was no surprise that some of the assholes that had been hounding my assistants over the years would be disgruntled at me finally giving in. Holly looked up at me, relief and embarrassment fighting for dominance in her gaze. She might feel some backlash from her peers for accomplishing what they couldn't, but I would protect her from anything they cared to throw at her.

Once she placed her hand in mine, a feeling of triumph swept over me, making me want to pound my chest in victory. It felt sweeter than the goal I had made with the entire stadium standing on their feet and cheering down the rafters. Before she could have a chance to change her mind, I began to pull her toward the elevators leading to the parking lot. I would let her drive her own car, I knew I'd have to give a little. I knew if I could show her I was reasonable and not just a caveman on hockey skates, she could trust me to be what she needed. I already needed her.

I pushed the button to the parking garage as soon as we stepped onto the lift and couldn't resist running my thumb over the delicate bones across the top of her hand again. I was already addicted to the feel of her skin. It was going to get worse; there was no doubt about that. I could feel the tether between us growing tighter and stronger the longer we were together. It had only been a few minutes, but somehow, it felt like an eternity at the same time. Maybe it was because she was the one I had been waiting for my entire life.

My grandfather had told me that the men in the family knew who their one was as soon as they laid eyes on them. I hadn't believed it, though I was fascinated by his stories when I was a little kid. After my dad left, my grandfather would shake his head and mutter, upset that his daughter hadn't found a man like the ones from our family line. Instead, I had to listen to my mom cry at night when she thought us kids were sleeping.

I swore that I would never have a relationship, not unless I were lucky enough to find what my grandfather had found with my grandmother. He loved her more than his own life. Everything he did was for her, and in return, she looked at him like he was her hero.

I looked down at Holly as the elevator came to a stop and could see it. The future would be beautiful. She would make a wonderful mother, and I would never do anything to hurt any of them. She would be everything to me, and I would make sure she never had a reason to cry.

"My car is right over there." She pointed a slightly trembling finger at a cute red BMW.

"Alright, sweetheart." I walked her over and waited until she slid in behind the wheel. "Meet me at the gate, and you can follow me to my apartment, okay?" I hesitated, even after she nodded, not wanting to lose sight of her, but finally backed away, knowing it wouldn't be for long.

Four

Holly

I had never been so nervous in my life. I did every breathing exercise I could think of, trying to get myself under control. I gripped the steering wheel hard as I followed the tail lights of the large SUV in front of me.

We were passing through the streets of downtown. The piles of snow recently plowed from the roads reflected the twinkling lights from the street lamps. The city was always decorated for the holidays, but during Christmas, they seemed to want to bring joy to every single person who passed through the streets. Even though I was never overly cheerful during the holidays, even I could appreciate the magical quality of the wonderland they created.

I wasn't letting my dad or his implied threat intrude tonight. I was nervous, but it had nothing to do with the job I had to do. It was about the man I would be alone with. I could see that he was interested in me as more than just a person conducting an interview. In fact, I was certain that my being a journalist was probably the one thing that had him thinking twice. Not that he seemed to have many second thoughts. From the moment he walked up to me, he had hardly taken his eyes off me.

As a girl so controlled by my parents, I didn't have the typical teenage years growing up. Though I went to a private high school, I was also tutored at home every day after school, whether I needed it or not. My parents didn't want to take any chances that I could fall behind, nor would they allow any distractions. When I wasn't being tutored or studying at home, I was at the office, learning about the business at my dad's side. There were no sports, friends, or parties. Certainly, no boyfriends. This would be the first time I would be alone with a man. Just the thought had me taking deep breaths, trying to cool my nervousness while I was also growing uncomfortably warm.

I wasn't sure what was going to happen once we got to his place. I think he mentioned a penthouse? But as I stared out my windshield at the merrily blinking lights, I decided that I would go with the flow. However the night went, I wouldn't fight it. Maybe it was the magic of Christmas being just days away, or perhaps my rebellious teenage years were finally catching up with me, but for once, I just wanted to live without thinking, planning, or considering the future.

I followed the SUV into an underground car park and waited while Trent parked for him to point me to a spot that I should park in. As soon as my car engine was turned off, he had my door open, a slow grin forming, turning his serious expression from the stadium into one of a happy little boy. It also brought out a crease in one cheek that wasn't quite a dimple but was close enough to one that I decided right then that's what it was.

He held out his hand to help me from my car like a gentleman. With one last steadying breath, I placed my hand in his and let him guide me from the vehicle. I realized he never dropped my hand as he led me toward the elevator. I darted a glance down. Yep, we were still connected. I wondered if he could feel the slight tremble in my palm. Oh no! What if he could feel how sweaty I was getting? How awful.

When he ushered me into the elevator, he had to let my hand go so I could enter before him. I hadn't expected the flash of disappointment in losing his grip on me, but I took the opportunity to quickly wipe my palm on my pants as inconspicuous as possible. When he looked down at me with a smile, I couldn't help melting inside and was so glad that I managed to keep my sigh contained. He was just so handsome. I knew I was here for an interview, but there was a palpable tension surrounding us. If I didn't know better, I'd think it was chemistry.

As soon as the door slid open with a ping, he retook my hand, and I was so glad I had wiped it off. We walked down a long hallway with only two doors on either side. It reminded me of an elegant and expensive hotel with beautiful artwork, a long table set against one of the walls with a crystal vase and fresh flowers. He led me to the door on the right, just past the table, and used his thumb on the biometric lock to open the door.

I had grown up in an expensive, sprawling home full of art and fancy furniture that I wasn't allowed to sit on or touch. This penthouse apartment was obviously expensive, but the decor was more along the lines of 'come in and sit down, enjoy the game'. An oversized black leather couch was sitting in front of the largest television screen I had ever seen.

There weren't any fancy paintings, no small Chippendale tables with gilded vases, just comfortable but very nice and high-quality furniture. The lights in the living room area were down low, but the light of the full moon provided plenty of light. My breath caught in my throat when I turned toward the window. It wasn't a mere window, though. It was floor-to-ceiling panes of glass that spanned the length of the room. In a daze, my feet carried me to the glass wall, not even noticing when he took my jacket and bag from me.

Without much thought, I placed my palms flat against the panes of glass and stared out at the night. With the multicolored lights covering the city below and the large, fat flakes that had begun to fall from the sky above, it was as if I were staring out into a dreamscape. Tears filled my eyes at the wondrous beauty of the scene.

"Hey," Trent was closer than I expected when I turned my head to face him. I had to blink several times to pull myself from the spell I had been under. "Are you okay, sweetheart?"

I smiled, tipping up the corners of my mouth, and lifted my hand to finally do what I had wanted to since I had seen him barreling down on me in that crowded hallway back at the stadium. With fascination, I smoothed my thumb over the crease between his eyebrows, watching with satisfaction as the line immediately disappeared at my touch.

"The view is beautiful," I whispered, finally meeting his eyes with mine, dropping my hand with embarrassment at touching him so freely without his permission. I had no excuse other than I had been so caught up in the moment.

He quickly grasped the hand I had just been touching him with and brought the fingers to his mouth, grazing his lips over the tips. "The most beautiful I have ever seen."

His eyes never left mine as he said the words. Somehow, the spell the view outside the apartment had weaved around me still worked its magic on me. Or it was the man causing my heart rate to escalate and a fuzzy sensation to fill my mind.

"Do you want to conduct your interview now?" His voice was deep, low, and rumbling over me, causing goosebumps to cover my arms.

I nodded, ready to agree to anything he suggested. He seemed to sense what was happening inside me because the next thing I knew, he had closed his blue eyes and groaned low and deep. When those eyes reopened, there was a new look in them, one that had fireworks shooting off in my belly. His pupils were dilated with a hungry gaze that had nothing to do with food, though he did look like he wanted to eat me.

"Tell me to stop, sweetheart." It was a plea, but his eyes begged me not to. He shouldn't have worried. I could no more ask him to stop than I could have told my heart to stop beating.

FIVE

I held my breath, waiting to hear her answer. I cupped her cheeks in my hands and just stared at her features, taking her in. She stared up at me with what I could only describe as an innocent desire. Her cheeks were rosy, her lips parted slightly, panting little puffs of air over my thumbs, causing me to give into my instincts. I ran the pad of one thumb over her plump bottom lip before putting pressure on it, pulling it down just slightly. When she darted out her little pink tongue to run over my thumb, I almost lost my control that was hanging by the thinnest thread.

I groaned at the sight, imagining that tongue all over me. "Sweetheart, I'm barely hanging on here. We can sit down, conduct your interview, and I can walk you to your car."

She swallowed, her eyes immediately changing from lust to fright as if she worried I would leave her. Maybe she thought I didn't want her. She couldn't be more wrong. I had never wanted anything more in my life. But this was a critical moment for both of us. As much as I wanted everything she had to give, I would never push her into it.

"You have to tell me, sweetheart." I didn't know what to say to her to make this easier. Anything I did from this point would feel like I was pressuring her. "I want you more than I could say. But it's your choice. Everything is your choice."

I dropped my hands, backed away one step, then two, and stood there, waiting with my heart ready to burst from anticipation. I watched as she swallowed again, panic written all over her face. She darted her eyes from the window to the door, then down to her feet. She continued to stare down at the floor for several long heartbeats. Then she squared back her shoulders, making a decision, and it was my turn to hold my breath. If she walked away, I would let her. It wouldn't be the last time I saw her, though. I would find her and court her the old-fashioned way if I needed to.

When she raised her head to look at me with her hazel eyes, the gold flecks shining in the dim lights, I knew she was mine.

"I want you, too." Her words were so low I could barely hear them in the silence of the apartment. But they were all I needed. Wordlessly, I stepped into her, picking up her slight weight. I grunted in approval when she wrapped her long legs around my waist. She was mine; she gave herself to me, and I would never let her go again.

I took her mouth in a heated kiss, never knowing it would heat my blood to the molten point as quickly as it did. With one press of her soft lips to mine, I was already done. I knew she was the one with one look. Now that I was touching her, tasting her, I was beyond the capability of rational thought beyond mine, mine, mine.

I swiftly carried her to our room, the room we would share from now on. I had never had a woman in my room. Hell, I had never had a woman, ever. I was never more glad of that fact until this moment. She was all I'd ever need, and I would ensure she never needed anything other than me.

I lay her back on my bed, admiring her hair shining in the dark, but I needed to see all of her. I reached over and switched on the lamp and nearly fell to my knees to worship at her side.

"I'm going to strip you now." I hardly recognized my own voice; it was so gruff and held a hint of the wildness I felt. I had to clench my fists repeatedly until I regained control before touching her. I never wanted to hurt her.

She rubbed her legs together as she watched me fighting with myself. She was panting, her small chest rising and falling rapidly as she licked her lips in anticipation. With jerky movements, I reached behind my head and yanked my T-shirt off, tossing it to the floor somewhere behind me, relishing in her swift intake of breath as I exposed my torso to my girl.

Finally, I knelt on the bed, caging her legs between mine, and bent to kiss her again, finding it difficult to stay away from her now that I tasted her for the first time. As I coaxed her mouth open to accept my tongue, I ran my hands up her sides and let my thumbs rub across the sides of her breasts. I didn't know which one of us moaned when I slid over her puckered nipples. It was probably both of us.

We were both so lost in the kiss and in the heat of the moment that when we pulled away to take her top over her head, we both blinked in surprise. Goosebumps dotted her skin from the cool air, but I could only stare, admiring her lovely curves. She was perfect. Every inch of her was absolutely gorgeous and perfect.

I bent down to one of the lace-covered peaks and sucked as much as I could into my mouth, grunting at the feel as she arched her back. It wasn't enough. I needed her skin, and I needed to feel every inch of her without any barriers. With a huff, I yanked down the cups, then gripping as gently as I could manage in my agitated state, I held both breasts and simply stared at the beautiful, rosy nipples that matched the color of the blush on her cheeks.

I licked and sucked, loving the way she writhed under me. "Sweetheart, are you okay?" It was hard, but I needed to check to make sure she was still with me. I knew I was going fast, but I wasn't sure I could slow down, not unless she asked me to.

"Please, don't stop," she moaned hoarsely. "Please! I need—I think I need more!"

I didn't know what brought this goddess into my life, but I was going to thank every deity that man has ever worshipped. As soon as I was done.

"Oh, sweetheart. I'm going to give you more. But I need you to tell me if I get too rough, okay? I need you to tell me so I don't hurt you." I pulled back, searching her face for any signs of fear.

Her eyes were bright, but she didn't look scared. She looked determined. When she raised her arms and put them around my shoulders, and pulled my head back down to her and growled, "I'm fine! I need you to trust that I'm good with this." I finally gave in to the instincts I had been holding back.

With a snarl, I pulled back from her grip and sat up. In swift, jerky movements, I had her pants undone and off her legs, taking the little lace panties with them. Seeing her bared to me was a sight I would remember and cherish forever.

"I need to taste you!" I growled as I buried my head in her heat, spreading her legs wide with my hands, holding her thighs to make room for my large shoulders.

"Oh, o-okay," she squealed as I gave the first long lick up her center and groaned against her, not wanting to move away from my new favorite meal. Over and over, I licked, feasting on every part of her, not letting a single inch escape. As I enjoyed her sounds, her writhing against me, I reached down to pop the button on my jeans, needing to let myself free from the confinement before my dick strangled. I couldn't remember being so hard or feeling so desperate to come. I stroked myself once, feeling the pre-come coating the head of my dick, but I immediately stopped. I wouldn't let my come go anywhere but inside or on her from now on. It all belonged to her.

When her thighs began to shake, I sank my tongue as deep inside her as possible before slipping back up to her gorgeous little clit and sucking hard. Her screams filled our bedroom as she tugged my hair. That was okay, though. She could rip it all out if she wanted to. It was hers now.

As soon as she fell back, limp against the pillows, I grinned at the satisfied little smile on her lips. It was a job well done. Now, I needed to see if I could make her scream in pleasure again while I was balls deep inside of her.

I shoved my jeans down, quickly kicked them off, and tugged my socks off, tossing them to the floor with everything else. I bent over her once again, holding my cock at her entrance, and waited for her to open her eyes for me. I needed to have her looking at me as I entered her for the first time. Maybe I wouldn't need her eyes in the future, but right now, I needed to see her and have her know it was me. I needed her to know that she belonged to me and I was hers.

When she blinked her eyes open, I reached between her breasts and popped the clasp there, helping her pull her arms free. All the while, my impatient dick rested right at her entrance. Every wriggle, every movement sent jolts of pleasure running down my spine, but I knew it was about to get so much better.

Once completely bared to each other in every way, I leaned down to kiss her tenderly. With our eyes on each other and our mouths touching softly, I pressed in slowly. When I had to press harder to gain entrance, I briefly squeezed my eyes shut at the overwhelming emotions filling me at the significance of the moment. I quickly opened them again, refusing to miss a single second.

With a final thrust and grunt, I was fully seated inside my girl.

"Mine," I snarled.

"Yours," she breathed with tears in her eyes.

I kissed the tears from her eyes and began to slide back out, only to thrust back in. Over and over, I brought us to new heights until we were both lost. Until we were both found again, by each other. When I spilled myself inside her clutching heat, and we were both panting, I smiled into her neck. We were finally one.

Six

HOLLY

I woke slowly, stretching my arms and feeling an ache I had never felt before. It took me several long blinks and looking around the unfamiliar bedroom before the night came back to me.

Trent had taken me two more times after that first one. All three had been beautiful. He made me feel special, cared for, loved. He cleaned me gently with a warm washcloth in between bouts of lovemaking. After the second time, we had taken a shower in which he carefully washed every inch of me. He had gently made love to me in the shower, holding me in his strong arms against the tile wall. When he was done after making me scream his name again, he gently cleaned me once more.

Then he dried me off with a warm towel before tucking me against his side under the covers. It was there that we finally talked. I suppose it could have been considered his interview. When I had told him so he laughed and said I could write anything I wanted about him. He also told me why he had always been so against reporters. His dad had been a journalist. When given an opportunity to follow a big story, he hadn't looked back at his family. He simply packed up and left, chasing the story. His mother had been left to take care of Trent and his siblings. It had made me cry for the little boy he had once been. I promised that I would never leave him the way his father had.

We fell asleep with Trent running his fingers gently through my hair. It was a peaceful moment, so magical. Everything he had told me made me feel like it was as special for him as it was for me. Like I was special to him.

I looked around, sitting up in his big bed while holding the sheet to my chest. I didn't know why I was alone and wondered where he was. It wasn't until I heard whistling and the sound of water that I realized he was taking a shower again. I giggled, imagining joining him in the bathroom. I could surprise him, maybe return the favor of going down on him the way he had on me the night before.

I was about to throw back the sheet when the bedroom door flew open, and a woman rushed in, looking upset. I pulled the sheet back to my chest with a small squeal, wondering what the hell this older woman was possibly thinking by barging in on Trent's bedroom.

She was older, probably close to my mother's age, and wearing a suit, her graying hair up in a bun. At first, I thought it had to be his mother, but I changed my mind when I got a good look at her. There was no way this woman was related to Trent. It wasn't until her words penetrated my shocked brain that the tears began to fall.

"Hurry up, girl! Didn't you hear me? Mr. Frost hates reporters. I need you up and out of this apartment right now before he comes back in here."

I sat there numb while listening to her and watching as she separated my clothes from his from where they were strewn all over the floor. She tossed them on the bed with disgust and glared at me as she continued to wait impatiently.

"Now!" She snapped, muttering under her breath as I slid out of the bed, still clutching the sheet to me. She rolled her eyes at my actions. "As if it's anything I haven't seen before. You think you are the only piece of ass Mr. Frost has had me eject from his home?"

I had to swallow back the sob her words brought as I reached out with shaky hands, grabbing my wrinkled slacks and sliding them over my legs. I had to wriggle into my bra without letting the sheet slip. Regardless of what this nasty woman had to say, I wouldn't let her see my naked body as she stood there with her arms crossed, glaring at me.

The whole time I got dressed, the tears refused to stop. I had believed everything he told me last night. I had believed that I was his first, the same as he was for me. It hurt more than anything to know that it was all a lie. I couldn't wrap my head around the fact that he had made me believe I was special, that what we had was special.

As I walked with her to the door, my arm held tightly in her grip, the pain in my chest was breaking my heart wide open. I could imagine the trail of blood I was leaving behind. When I looked back toward the bedroom I had such a wonderful night in, I was almost surprised that the carpet was still pristine.

At the door, she grabbed my bag from the hook without handing it to me. When we could hear the water from the shower shut off, her eyes grew panicked before she barked at me in a low, menacing tone.

"It's time to leave! Now! I can't have you here when he gets out!"

With a yank, she pulled me from the apartment before I could even think to call out to Trent, to demand answers from him. She tugged me all the way to the elevator, shoving me on and repeatedly smashing her finger into the button. I wanted to tell her that it wouldn't make the elevator move any faster with as much snark as I could muster, but before I could even try, my will crumbled. It was over, and there was nothing left to be done about it.

She escorted me the entire way to my car, standing there with her arms crossed over her chest. When I started to close the door, her hand shot out, stopping it mid swing, and gave me one last warning.

"Don't contact Mr. Frost again. Stay away from here, and don't try to talk to him at the stadium, or he will have charges of stalking brought against you. Frankly, you are lucky all he did was fuck you, considering how much he hates reporters."

With those final words, she allowed me to shut the door. With numb fingers, I started the engine, put it in drive, and drove away, leaving my tattered heart all over the tarmac.

When I got home, I slipped through the door, hoping to avoid my parents, but it was the theme of the day to have my heart stomped to bits. As soon as my dad saw me enter, looking like I had just spent the night rolling around in some man's bed, his face grew redder than I had ever seen it.

"Where have you been?" he demanded as soon as he saw me.

"I, uh, I spent the night with someone." I couldn't bring myself to admit with whom or that I was used by someone who made me believe what we had was love.

My mother stood next to him, grasping her pearls in shock. I wanted to snort at the picture she made. "I can't believe you are crawling in looking like—like, I just can't!" She clenched her pearls tighter. "Did anyone see you like this?" She turned to my dad. "Harry! What would the neighbors think?"

My dad just continued to stare at me with disgust. "Did you get the interview?"

Of course, that was all that mattered to him. I thought about it, thought of our quiet talk in the middle of the night. I could say yes; I could give all the information Trent had told me about his father and his mother, but no matter what had happened, I couldn't bring myself to do it. I shook my head and swallowed. "No, he, uh, doesn't talk to the press. He hates reporters."

My dad narrowed his eyes at me before taking a step closer. "You had one job to do. You only had to prove yourself to this family and this company. Since you can't complete a simple task like conducting an interview, I can't see myself leaving you in charge of my company. There is no place for you here. Just another disappointing daughter." He shook his head, the disappointment and disgust clear.

He turned away from me, giving me his back, and strode off toward his office with my mother trailing after him, wailing about the disgrace she would face if anyone had seen me this morning.

My shoulders slumped even further as I turned toward the stairs. I climbed them on numb feet, pulling myself forward with every step with my hand on the railing. It wasn't until I entered my bedroom that the sob that had been locked in my chest finally escaped.

The entire time I packed a suitcase full of my everyday clothes, leaving behind the suits I had been forced to wear to the office, the tears continued to fall, making me need to swipe my eyes to see. Once I packed my suitcase, I picked up my phone and keys. On the way back down the staircase, I called my sister.

"Helen?" My voice was hoarse, the pain evident in my tone. "Can I come to you?"

"Oh, Holly Berry! They kicked you out, too, didn't they?" I couldn't speak, just a sound like a whine and a gurgle coming from my throat at her question. "Of course, you can come here. You never have to ask."

SEVEN

FOUR YEARS LATER

HOLLY

"T.J.! Slow down, Mister, or you're going to bust your head open!" My little guy was as rambunctious as any three-year-old little boy could be. He certainly kept me on my toes. He had two modes— asleep and running. But no matter how often I had to bite my fist from completely freaking out when he did his thing, I wouldn't change it for the world.

Being a young, single mother wasn't exactly what I had expected from my life, but I wouldn't change it for the world. It was often the only thing that got me through the long days. Though my nights were lonely, and I had to hide my tears from my sister, knowing I was a mother helped in every way. Looking at my son, I could never forget his father. The shattered pieces of my heart would never be whole again, but the precious gift of motherhood held at least the pieces together.

"Come on, sweet boy, we are meeting Auntie Helen at the mall so you can tell Santa what a good boy you've been." And he really had been.

I helped him slide his thin coat on. It was nothing like what we would have had to bundle up in if we still lived back east. The weather was so much warmer, and the winters were pretty mild, with no snow in the city. Since moving to California, more than the weather has changed.

It took me longer than it should have to realize I was pregnant. Three months had passed before I realized that my nausea was caused by more than heartache. By the time I had gone to the doctor and received the news of what I was carrying, I was already in my second trimester. I had tried to call Trent's publicist, hoping to get through to Trent. I had an overwhelming need to let him know that he was going to be a father. Instead of being able to talk to him, I was met with a stone wall. The same woman who had ejected me so harshly from his penthouse that day was the one who answered my call. She wouldn't even let me leave a message.

It took days for Helen to calm me down after the phone call that resulted in more threats. This time, it was a slander lawsuit as well as a stalking charge. Helen ended up having to take me to the doctor, where I had been told the harsh truth. If I didn't start taking better care of myself, I would lose the pregnancy. From then on, I had to change my focus. I couldn't even hear about Trent, let alone look him up online. If I still softly cried into my pillow at night, at least I was eating and putting on the weight I had lost.

Once I got T.J. buckled into his car seat, I climbed in and started up the car. I was grateful that my parents had let me leave without a fuss, not trying to make me leave my car behind. It was as if they just wanted to erase me from their lives, the same way they had my sister. Luckily, the car had been new when I left, barely a few months old. It was still in excellent condition, so I didn't have to worry about carrying precious cargo in it.

I looked in the rearview mirror to see the little, dark head bent over a book as he scanned the pictures. I couldn't help but smile at seeing him there. I could easily picture that it was Trent when he was a little boy.

"Are you ready, little man?" I called as I began to back out of the driveway.

"Ready, momma!" Ugh, his little voice that couldn't quite pronounce all his words perfectly just yet melted me every time.

It didn't take as long as it usually did with the kind of traffic the city typically had. Before too long, I cruised the lanes of the mall parking lot, trying to find an empty parking space. I finally gave up and parked in the very back. It wasn't as if the weather was freezing. We would be able to manage a brisk walk in the cool air.

I helped T.J. hop down from the car, and we both started walking, holding hands and giggling at silly jokes. The closer we got to the mall entrance, the more excited T.J. got, bouncing up and down and beginning to beg to see Santa. I had my concerns about how it would go, though. Last year, he had screamed bloody murder the second he was near the big guy. I ended up holding him up on the other side of the Christmas display and took a selfie with Santa in the background.

"Come on, momma! I want to see Santa! Come on!" He began pulling me to get me to move faster, making me laugh at his eagerness.

"Slow down, little man! There are a lot of people here. We don't want to run anybody over, do we?" That reminder got him to slow down fractionally as he jutted out his lip in a little pout. It didn't last long once he heard the cheery Christmas music that let us know the Christmas village was close.

He started yanking on my hand again, yelling for me to hurry. His little body could dart between other shoppers, whereas I had to mumble apologies as I tried to squeeze through them. My grip on his hand started to slip, and my panic began to rise. It was so crowded that if I lost sight of him, I would have a hard time finding him again.

"T.J.! Stop!"

As soon as I called out, I was met by a wall of teenagers all grouped together. He slipped right out of my hand and through the small gap between two girls carrying armfuls of shopping bags. I shoved my way through, elbowing past the girls, my eyes frantically searching for his little dark head.

"Hey!"

"Watch it, lady!"

I ignored the angry curses of the teenagers as I stumbled past them. I swiveled my head back and forth but couldn't see him anywhere. I started to run in the direction of the Christmas village, certain that was where he was headed, but the closer I got, the more bodies there were to get through.

"T.J.!" I called out for him, my heart pounding painfully in my chest. It was my worst nightmare. I couldn't lose my baby. "Oh, god," I moaned in frustration, fear clogging my throat. "T.J.!"

Finally, a small break in the crowd opened up, and I saw my little boy standing still, staring up at a man with his hand on my son's shoulder. My feet froze in place, unable to move.

I watched as my three-year-old son stood staring up at a man who looked exactly like him. They had the same dark hair and the same blue eyes. And the same crease that was almost, but not quite, a dimple in one cheek.

The man stood staring down at T.J. with a look of confusion. Then I watched as his head slowly raised until his eyes were on me. His expression was unreadable, his face carefully blank. Then his head slowly lowered again, taking another long look at his son.

EIGHT

TRENT

"I know, Mom. I don't like being away right now, either. But I promise I will be back by Christmas dinner. No, Mom. I don't want to meet anyone. No, I don't care if she's a nice girl. I told you I'm not interested..." I pinched the bridge of my nose as I stood at the jewelry counter, waiting for the salesman to box up the necklace I had just bought as a Christmas gift for the woman who was going to make me hang up on her again.

I knew she was worried about me. Hell, everyone had been worried about me for four long years. But I wasn't giving in. I had no desire to meet someone new. I never will. I had my one and lost her. She was it for me. There could never be another to take her place.

What hurt the most was that she had simply vanished. I had gotten up to take a shower, planning on taking my girl out for a nice breakfast and a day of fun, just getting to know each other better. I was already making plans to take her to meet my mom. I didn't know what her plans were for Christmas, but I was sure that we would spend it together no matter what.

I never found out what had caused her to run that day, but in my mind, it didn't matter. We were meant to be together, and nothing could keep us apart. If I needed to convince her or calm her fears we were moving too fast, I was prepared to do just that. I wasn't upset at her for running, but the longer I searched for her with no answers as to where she had gone, the harder it got to breathe.

The first thing I did was find out from Fred where Holly worked. When I stormed into the building expecting to find her, it was to be told that she no longer worked there. When I hired a private detective to trace her and found out where she lived, I was told by a snotty, rich housewife that she didn't have any daughters. At my confused look, she sniffed, then slammed the door in my face.

After finding out her father was actually the owner of the company she used to work for, I made an appointment to speak to him. The only way I could even get him to agree was to promise an interview. He ended up being as unhelpful as his wife. All he would tell me was that Holly had failed to fulfill what had been required of her and that she was let go.

I sat there, giving him a stunned look of disbelief. "You fired your daughter?

He grunted and steepled his hands together. "I don't expect you to understand. Children are meant to carry on our legacy. When they let you down and are nothing but a disappointment, their worth becomes minimal." I could feel my blood pressure rise with every word he spoke and had to clench the armrests of the chair I was in to keep myself from lunging for his throat. "Perhaps one day you will have children of your own. Then you will understand what it's like to expect greatness and only receive mediocrity."

"Whatever children Holly and I have together will be perfect no matter what they choose to do with their lives. I would only be grateful they exist at all," I seethed between gritted teeth and a clenched jaw.

Mr. Fields merely scoffed and waved my words away with a pass of his hand through the air. I stood to my feet, my hands clenched into fists at my side. He looked up at me with an irritated glance. "What are you doing? We need to conduct your interview for the article."

"Consider this another disappointment in your mediocre life."

With those parting words, I left the building, refusing to return even after he called after me. I then left strict instructions with my assistant to ignore all phone calls unless it was to give me information about Holly.

I slipped the phone into my pocket after gaining a disgruntled agreement from my mom that there wouldn't be any surprise guests over for Christmas. I took the handles of the small gift bag with a nod of thanks and stepped out of the store and back into the noise of the crowded mall. The jewelry store was right next to the Christmas village, and all around me were the shouts of excited little children and tired parents begging them to be patient. I snorted at the thought. That line was long, and I couldn't imagine how long the wait to see Santa was.

I was making my way through the crowd easily enough; my size and height had advantages sometimes when a small body collided with my legs. I reached out a hand to steady the tiny kid, not wanting him to fall and get hurt. I looked down at him to make sure he was okay when my body froze.

He looked up at me with big blue eyes and smiled, a slight crease in his cheek. It was eerie, almost like looking at a picture of myself from when I was little. Mom still had many pictures of me and my siblings on the walls from all the stages of our childhoods, so I had seen myself plenty of times to know that this kid could have been my much younger doppelganger.

Something about the situation itched at my brain. I wanted to ask him who he was and how old he was when I felt eyes burning into me. It was harder than I would have imagined looking away from the kid, but when I lifted my head and glanced over to see the woman standing just a few feet away, seeming as if she were about to burst into tears, my world stopped.

When I glanced back down at the little boy again, the world jerked back into motion. I dropped to one knee, trying and failing to get on the same level as the boy. Pieces of my broken heart slowly started to slide back into place as I took in every inch of him as he stood there and smiled at me with that little half-dimple in his cheek.

"Hi! I'm T.J.!" His voice was that same little voice that young children have, and I felt my lip twitch, wanting to smile. I cleared my throat, but all I could do was rasp out my question.

"What does T.J. stand for?"

"Trent Junior. What's your name?"

I nearly choked on the golf ball lodged in my throat as I tried to answer, but my voice failed me. As I opened and closed my mouth, willing sound to come out, the voice I had heard in my dreams for the past four years came from right behind my son.

"His name is Trent, sweetheart. He's your daddy."

I lifted my eyes to look at the woman I had been missing, who I never stopped looking for. She looked the same but different. Her hair was longer, and she was thinner than before. I frowned at her. She was already thin four years ago, and she didn't have weight to lose. Was she not taking care of herself? I saw the circles under her eyes that told me she hadn't been sleeping well, and I wanted to tuck her into bed and hold her all night just to make sure she got the rest she obviously needed.

Her face flushed, and she looked down at the floor, biting her lip in obvious distress. She was wringing her hands in front of her, her fingers flexing as if she wanted to reach out and grab our son.

I started to speak, to tell her that we should leave, to go somewhere quiet to talk. We had many things to discuss, four years to go over, and plans to make for the future. But a woman's voice called Holly's name just as a little girl yelled, "Mommy!"

NINE

Trent was here. Oh my god. How could that be? Out of all the places to finally see him again, it was in the middle of the mall's Christmas village. And our son just happened to run right into him. What were the chances? They had to be astronomical.

I gripped my fingers together tightly, trying to contain the urge to snatch T.J. back to me. I wasn't afraid of Trent; I would trust him with my life. But that was my little boy, one of my reasons for living. I also had no idea what was going through Trent's mind. I didn't know if he hated me before, and now that he found out that I kept his children from him, he might never forgive me. I could try to explain that I tried to reach him, but would he understand?

"Mommy!" Angelica ran up to me, wrapping her little arms around my legs, beaming up at me. "We found you!"

I ran my fingers through her long hair and gave her a shaky smile. "You did," I said with a whisper, then looked back over at

Trent to see another stunned look cross his face. Angelica turned
to see what I was looking at and, spotting her brother, bounced
over to him enthusiastically.

"Teej! We found you!" She finally noticed Trent kneeling on
the floor and turned to him with her crooked smile, the crease in
the opposite cheek from her brother's. "Hi, who are you?"

Before anyone else could speak, T.J. spoke up. "He's
Daddy."

A choked sound came from next to me as Helen came to a
stop. "That—that's..."

"That's Trent," I whispered.

Trent looked up at me from where he'd been glancing back
and forth between the twins. He had tears in his eyes that he
didn't bother to blink away as he stared up at me with what I
could only describe as awe. "You gave me twins?"

I nodded, feeling myself choke up, knowing that if I tried to
speak, it would come out as a sob. This was what I had dreamed of
for so long, to finally see the man I had been in love with and tell
him the truth.

"Listen here, Trent, those are Holly's kids. She carried them
alone. She's raised them alone with only help from me. Where
have you been this whole time she needed you, huh? Do you think
you can just waltz back into her life and lay claim to those kids?
You must have been knocked over the head too many times with a
hockey puck..."

"Helen!" I grabbed her arm and tugged her back from where
she had advanced on Trent, looking like she was ready to do bodily
harm to him. "It's okay," I said softly as she turned to look at me
in shock.

"You can't be serious, Holly Berry! This man..."

"Didn't know he had children. He has a right to see them, you
know that."

She grunted and crossed her arms over her chest, and glared

back at Trent, still kneeling in front of the kids, but with a stricken look on his face. Oh god.

"Why don't we go somewhere quieter so we can talk?" I offered and reached out my hands for the children to take. When they stepped away from him to come to my side, he looked like he wanted to pull them back.

He nodded his head, looking down at the floor, causing my heart to ache in my chest. I wanted to tell him everything was alright, but was it? We needed to talk so badly. We both needed to explain our ends of things.

He stood up, and as he reached his full height, both children craned their heads back to take him in. Considering I was taller than average for a woman, the kids were above average in height for their ages. But standing next to him, he might as well be a giant to them. I could already see the hero worship start to form in their eyes.

I gave him a small smile and turned to walk back the way we had come. I expected the children to complain since they had their hearts set on seeing Santa, but neither of them complained as they walked with me, each of them turning back to look at their father as he followed closely behind us. Then I felt a tug on my hand once we made it to the doors we had entered when we'd first arrived just a few short minutes ago. It seemed like an eternity had passed. Between my frantic terror of losing sight of T.J. and then seeing Trent again after all these years, I felt as if I'd aged a good twenty years.

I stopped to look down at our son's face as he looked up at me with big eyes. His voice was firm and resolute when he spoke, making me swallow back a fresh wave of tears. "Momma, I want Daddy to walk me."

I looked over at Angelica, because whatever one twin wanted, the other was sure to follow. As expected, Angelica started bouncing on her toes. "I want to walk with Daddy, too!" I glanced back at Trent to see he had stepped up close behind us, likely concerned about what could be the matter. He swallowed hard and nodded, holding out his large hands. The twins eagerly let go of mine and reached for his, matching grins on their faces.

Trent looked at me with part fear, part pride and I had to fight a smile. I turned to lead the way to my car, knowing that he wouldn't let anything happen to our babies. Helen quickly came up next to me. I knew she had a lot to say about the matter. Though I valued her opinion and appreciated her more than I would ever be able to express, I wasn't sure how to tell her that the whole situation was between Trent and me. However, I would hear her out because I respected her. Ultimately, any decisions made wouldn't be hers.

My heart was so confused. I had never stopped yearning for him, but a part of me was scared that he might not be the same man I once knew. I couldn't help fearing he might try to take my children from me. What if he had someone new? What if he were married and would want to introduce the twins to his wife and have her be their new mother? I tried to shake the negative thoughts away. I couldn't let myself go down that hole.

Helen cleared her throat and leaned closer, her voice lowered so Trent and the kids couldn't hear her over their excited chatter. "Are you sure about this, Holly Berry?"

"He's their father," I whispered.

"But does he deserve to be in their lives? In your life?" She pressed.

I gave her a sharp look from the corner of my eye. "I won't keep them from him." My tone was harsh and insistent.

She pressed on despite the barely concealed warning. "Okay, but Holly, you have options. You could get a lawyer and start working on a custody agreement, visitations."

I knew she was right, but in my heart, I knew that wasn't what was good for any of us. I just shook my head, and when I stopped next to my car, I looked her in the eye and said, "No."

She sighed with an expression of understanding and held out her hand. "Then why don't you let me take the kids for dinner and ice cream? You two can go to the house and talk everything out while we are gone." She looked back at the trio as they finally caught up and then turned back to me with a half smile. "I'm sure you guys have much to talk about that the little crotch goblins shouldn't hear."

I just stared at my sister, speechless, for once, unable to get onto her for referring to my kids that way. T.J. did it for me instead.

"Don't call us cotch gobbins!"

At the same time, Angelica started cheering, "Ice cweam!"

TEN

TRENT

Holly stood beside me, staring at her car's taillights as her sister drove off with the kids. For a second, I had been tempted to snatch them back before she could take them, not wanting to let them out of my sight now that I had found them. But I had looked at Holly, looking small and conflicted as she peeked at me from under her lashes, and I knew that her sister was doing us a favor.

I held out my arm, gesturing toward the area I had parked in, and we began walking side by side. I desperately wanted to take her hand, hold it securely in mine as I had with the twins I had already fallen hopelessly in love with. How could I not? They had come from the woman I had known in an instant was supposed to be mine. But peering down at her, I wasn't sure she was ready for that closeness yet. Not until we talked everything out. Once we had answers, there would be no holding back. I would never let her go again.

"You bought jewelry."

Her softly spoken words pulled me from my thoughts of all the ways I could tie her to me permanently, not the least of which was to put another baby in her belly. I held out the small bag I had forgotten I held again after my daughter handed it back to me, from when she'd been swinging it as we walked. "Yeah, it's a bracelet."

I was so wrapped up in the fantasy of seeing her round with my baby that I almost missed the wave of pain she tried to hide on her beautiful face. I stopped and turned to her, making her stop to look up at me. I placed a finger under her chin so she couldn't look away when I told her the truth. "It's a Christmas present for my mom." I rubbed a thumb over her bottom lip, unable to resist the pull to her and my need. "There's never been anyone but you."

Her big hazel eyes looked up at me, and though I could see the doubt there, I could also see the hesitant hope. It was enough to work with. I reluctantly dropped my hand, this time claiming hers, unwilling to let doubts creep in and try to ruin that hope. As we walked, I squeezed her hand gently. "She's going to love you and the kids, you know." It was the absolute truth. Mom already knew everything there was to tell her about Holly. After she had disappeared, I had become so sullen she had forced me to tell her why. I knew she would have questions, but Mom had a big heart and would never hold whatever caused Holly to leave against her.

Holly didn't answer me as we reached the car, and that was okay. She would see in time. I helped her into her seat and pulled the strap over her chest, swallowing at the memory of those luscious breasts and wondering how much they had changed after being pregnant. I wondered if she had breastfed and how she had done during her pregnancy. I wanted to know everything and had to fight back the emotions that started filling me at the thought of missing out on everything that I rightfully should have been a part of since the beginning.

I pushed it all back and stood up from the car, shutting the door firmly before rounding the car to the driver's side. Being angry at the situation didn't stop my cock from hardening while being so close to her body again, though, and I had to adjust myself to a more comfortable position while I crossed behind the rental car.

I didn't ask her where to go. I just started driving to my hotel, needing to be alone with her and ensuring there was no way for us to be interrupted. She didn't say a word, seemingly lost in thought as I took the short drive. It didn't take long before I pulled up in front of the hotel and climbed out of the car in front of the valet stand. The young guy wearing a red vest had already opened my girl's door, but I stopped him before he could take her hand to help her out.

"I've got her," I growled, not looking back at him as I tossed him my keys and reached in to take her hand.

"That wasn't nice," she murmured under her breath as she tossed the kid a grateful smile.

"No one touches you but me." I knew I had already been possessive of her before, but now that I had found her again, I was realizing that I couldn't take the idea of another man touching her, however innocent it might be. I didn't know if those feelings of possessiveness would fade, but I didn't care. Holly was mine.

The ride to the top floor was tense and quiet, and my hands were clenched as I watched Holly draw into herself as if waiting for the executioner. She either had a story to tell that I wouldn't like, or she was expecting one. All I wanted was to get it out of the way so we could move on. I needed her like I needed air to breathe.

As soon as I swung the door open for her to enter first, all the control that I had been holding onto tightly broke, and I tossed the jeweler's bag on the nearest surface and stalked to my girl where she huddled protectively, her arms around her waist and her eyes watching me warily.

My hands went to my T-shirt first, ripping it over my head,

baring my toned torso to her. I didn't stop moving toward her as her eyes grew wide. I would have thought she was scared, but when she licked her lips, I knew that it was more than that. She wanted me as much as I wanted her.

"Trent," she gasped as I wrapped my arms around her waist and tugged her hard into me. I felt her breasts crush against my chest, and I let out a harsh moan at the contact. "What are you doing? We are supposed to talk." Her head dropped back to stare up at me, her pupils dilated with the desire she couldn't hide.

"We can talk later," I growled. "I need you now." My lips crashed onto hers, her soft lips pressing hard against mine. After licking along her mouth I raised my head long enough to let her see the full force of what I was feeling. "I need you now, sweetheart. I can't go another minute without you."

She wrapped her arms around my shoulders, her hands tangling in the hair at the back of my head as she went up on her tiptoes. "I need you, too."

Her whispered words against my lips were all the green light I needed to crush her body against mine and show her everything I felt. All the hurt and pain from losing her, all the shock and joy of finding her again, along with children I hadn't known we made together. And even some anger, not necessarily at her, but at the situation.

I held her body against mine, pulling us so close together that not even air was welcome between us. "I missed you so much." My words were whispered along her soft skin as I kissed my way down her neck and to her chest. When I ran out of flesh to taste, I growled and yanked her top up, pulling her arms up with my jerky movements. As soon as she was bared to me, I stared, taking in every inch of her, and it wasn't enough. I needed her completely naked, with no obstructions from getting to what I needed.

Her bra was discarded as roughly as her shirt, and I finally stopped before bringing my hands up to cup her gorgeous tits.

They had changed, grown just a bit, but I had the memory of what she had looked like four years ago seared into my brain. Her nipples were darker, too, and all I could do was swallow back the lump in my throat at remembering that she had been pregnant and given birth to my child—children without me.

I ran my thumb over one of her dusky nipples, feeling it tighten under my caress, and looked up into her eyes, filled with desire and a hint of self-consciousness. With our gazes on each other, I lowered my head to finally taste her there again, immediately sucking her puckered nipple into my mouth. I relished in her quiet moans of pleasure and held her close as she gripped onto my hair, holding me to her.

It wasn't enough. It would never be enough.

With a grunt, I pulled away, hating to leave but knowing there was more to be experienced together. I dropped to my knees, my hands immediately going to her jeans and popping the button. In one quick movement, I tucked my fingers into her waistband and yanked, making sure to get her panties at the same time. I pulled her jeans down to her thighs, and her hands immediately went to her stomach, shielding herself from me.

I glanced up at her face to see that vulnerability I had seen a glimpse of when I had bared her breasts. I took her hands gently in mine and moved them slowly but firmly to her sides, watching her face as I did. She squeezed her eyes shut, not wanting to see my reaction to the changes in her body. I lowered my gaze until I was looking directly at her abdomen and caught my breath.

Though she was still thin, thinner than she really should be, the flesh there wasn't quite as firm. Lines crossed her belly from her belly button down to the soft thatch of hair. Across the bottom of her abdomen, just above that hair, was a medical scar. The sight brought moisture to my eyes, along with that familiar pang of regret that I hadn't been there to watch her stomach grow and stretch. I leaned in, kissed each mark that scarred her stomach, and paused over the cesarean scar.

"You are a goddess. You made my children in here," I said as I caressed her soft flesh, feeling the uneven texture under my fingertips. "You held life inside of you. You have never been more beautiful to me than you are right now," I kissed her again before climbing back to my feet and taking her face in my hands.

I wiped the tears tracing down her cheeks and kissed her gently. "Thank you for having my children." I pulled back to look at her hazel eyes, the gold shining in the tears that filled them. "But, sweetheart? I'm going to need to get you pregnant again so I can experience it all with you this time."

She let out a breathy sob as she wrapped her arms around me and kissed me. It was the first kiss she'd initiated since we'd found each other again in that crowded mall. When our kiss ended, I tugged her until she fell back onto the mattress. I removed her shoes first, then finished removing her pants, finally stopping once she was completely naked from head to toe.

"You're so beautiful. You take my breath away," I said, meaning every word. My chest ached so much from taking her in that I had to rub the pain there with the palm of my hand. "I don't know why we lost each other, but Holly," I looked up to meet her eyes, letting her see the seriousness of my words. "I will never let you or our children go again. Nothing else matters but you. I know I have my hockey career, but I will break my contract tomorrow just to make sure I never live a day without you again. I couldn't take it, sweetheart. I need you with me."

ELEVEN

HOLLY

With all that he needed to say out of the way, Trent took his own clothes off with as much urgency as he had stripped me. I smiled as he put a knee to the bed and crawled over me. I welcomed him into my arms and legs, ready to welcome him back into my body. I was still scared to let him back into my heart, but I knew he wouldn't allow me to hold back from him. Truthfully, I didn't want to. I wanted the dream that had started from the moment we met. I wanted that promise of forever to come true.

When he placed the tip of himself at my entrance, I held my breath. When he pushed inside me slowly, I squeezed my eyes closed and tipped my head back on the bed, gasping toward the ceiling. He was a big man, and it had been four long years. But the pleasure was nearly overwhelming as I fit every thick inch of him, sliding inside until his pelvis pressed firmly against mine.

As he held still, I opened my eyes, panting from the unbeliev-able fullness and the euphoria of having him inside me again. He was looking down at me, watching my every reaction, looking on edge.

"I'm okay," I whispered, reaching up to cup his stumbled jaw. "You can move."

And he did. I hadn't thought anything could top our first time together. But I had been wrong. In long strokes that got increasingly faster and harder, I was on the edge before I could prepare myself for the massive wave of intense pleasure that washed over me, threatening to drown me in ecstasy.

"Fuck! You feel so good, I can't... " He grunted as my channel pulsed around him, holding him tightly. "Fuck!" He roared as he ground his pelvis against mine. As I felt him throb inside me and the warmth from his release fill me up, I closed my eyes, basking in what I thought I'd never be able to experience again as long as I lived.

A moment of panic began to fill me at the thought of getting pregnant again after what we'd just done. I couldn't go through that again. As much as I love my babies and wouldn't change their existence for the world, I didn't want to have another pregnancy and childbirth alone.

He must have felt the way my body stiffened as the worry crept in. I knew my eyes had likely gone round and frightened. He cupped my cheek, his chest still heaving with the exertion and from his powerful release, and seared me with his heavy gaze.

"Hey," he whispered, rubbing his nose against mine before pulling back slightly so he could keep eye contact. "I'm here, and I meant what I said. You and the kids are mine, and I won't let you go again."

My lips trembled as everything that was swirling through my head threatened to take me under. His eyes softened, and he studied my expression.

"Maybe you should tell me what happened that morning?" His words were still soft, but I could see that, as scared as I was, he was holding on to his own vulnerabilities. I nodded my head and shut my eyes as I thought back to that day. It didn't take much to recall the memory. It had stayed fresh in my mind, often playing like a reel in my head as I lay in bed at night.

"I woke up and heard you in the shower. I was about to get up to join you... " I trailed off and swallowed hard, needing to look away, but his blue eyes kept mine captive. "A woman entered the bedroom as I was getting up."

He jerked back, a look of shock swiftly taking over the softness. "A woman was in my apartment?" His tone was incredulous. I nodded my affirmation. "But there are only three women that had ever been there other than you." He looked away, staring at the wall above my head, thinking. I narrowed my eyes at his words. I knew he had a past before me, and though he'd indicated I was the only woman he'd been with, I didn't like the implications that he had women over.

"My mother was still in another state, and my housekeeper wasn't supposed to be there for at least a few days. Only my publicist, Nancy, would have had any reason to stop by." He stopped abruptly and swung his head back in my direction. "Older woman, probably hasn't smiled since the Great Depression?"

I didn't want to laugh since we were discussing a serious matter, but his fury and description were almost too much. I stifled my giggle, biting my lip when he narrowed his eyes. "Yeah. I didn't catch her name, though, as she watched me dress and escorted me out of your apartment, threatening to slap me with a restraining order if I ever tried to contact you again." By the time I was done summing up the encounter, all humor had fled.

In a heartbeat, Trent was up off the bed, and I immediately felt the loss of him. It wasn't just his warmth I missed; it was his body pressed close to mine, losing his presence inside me as he pulled out to begin pacing the hotel room. I grabbed the bed cover and pulled it over my nakedness. I watched, fascinated, as Trent lost his mind.

"What the actual fuck!" he growled, yanking on his hair. His fast strides from one end to the other of the room had his cock bouncing against his thighs. I couldn't help but stare at the sight and squeeze my thighs together, feeling the wetness of us combined leaking out of me. It was somehow gross and erotic at the same time. But even though the cold moisture was borderline uncomfortable, I couldn't tear my eyes away from his body.

He stopped and turned back to face the bed. As I watched, that cock that had been inside me just moments ago began to harden and lift from where I had been watching it swinging.

"Sweetheart, seeing you staring at me with that hungry look on your face is going to make me need to take you again," he growled. He took a step toward me, and I began to pant. "I need to get to the bottom of this shit, Holly." He reached down and slowly stroked his cock as I watched, a needy whimper escaping my parted lips. He groaned, then turned away to stalk over to the desk where he had thrown the room keycard, phone, and jewelry bag. "As much as I want to say fuck it and give you what your eyes are begging for, I need to fix this problem so it never happens again."

He punched a few buttons on his phone, then paused, making me finally tear my gaze away from his magnificent cock and look up at his face. He was looking at me, a question sitting there in his gaze. "Did you try to contact me when you found out you were pregnant?"

I knew why he was asking, not taking offense. I frowned as the despair I had felt after making that phone call returned. "Yes. The same woman who had thrown me out answered. She told me she would charge me with defamation for slander if I ever accused you of fathering a child with me again and promised to follow through on the restraining order for stalking. I—I didn't know what to do."

He nodded once and jerked his gaze back to the phone, pulling it up to his ear. After a few seconds, he barked into the phone. "You're fired. And let me tell you something that isn't a threat, that I will damn well follow up on. If you ever speak to me or the mother of my children again, you will never work in this industry again." He paused, then growled. "You had no right to make that decision. You knew she had been in my bed and should have asked me instead of deciding I wanted to get rid of her. She wasn't a one-night stand, damn it, Nancy! That was the love of my life, and you threw her out like garbage. Because of you, I lost four years with her and my children." He huffed and pinched the bridge of his nose. "There is no excuse that you could ever give that could make this even remotely okay. You're fired, Nancy. Goodbye."

He punched the button on the phone and tossed it back down. I watched it slide against the smooth wooden surface. All this because of some woman who thought she was doing the right thing? There was still something that needed answering, though.

"If you really didn't want me gone, why didn't you try to contact me?" My voice was small, unsure if I wanted to hear that he hadn't tried.

He stalked back over to the bed, where I clutched the blanket to my chest in tight fists, blinking up at him with watery eyes.

"I did," he growled. "I hired a private detective. I went to your old job. It wasn't until I figured out who your father was that I thought I'd found you. But that piece of shit basically said he didn't have a daughter anymore." He jerked the cover from me as I gasped. Then he caged me in with his large body before settling his hips against mine, his erection rubbing against my sensitive clit. "I kept searching, but you had disappeared."

I whimpered. "I moved in with my sister and work from home

as Helen's personal assistant. She pays me in cash and lets me and the kids live there rent-free." I tossed back my head as he slid inside me again. "Your PI didn't find my medical records?"

He grunted as he bottomed out inside me. "Not that he ever told me," he snarled, pulling back his hips and thrusting deep and hard. "Never again. Do you hear me, Holly? No one is ever going to keep us apart ever again."

All I could do was dig my fingernails into his shoulders and nod.

Epilogue

HOLLY

Watching Trent and the kids get to know each other was the most beautiful and the most heartbreaking thing. Beautiful because they fell into their relationships perfectly, as if they had never been apart. It was as if they had always known each other, effortlessly welcoming each other into their hearts.

It was sad because they had been denied beginning their new bonds for no good reason. Nancy had tried making excuses, but Trent refused to hear her out. When she hadn't stopped calling, he got pissed. When she tried showing up at his penthouse apartment, where the kids and I had moved in with him within two days, he'd almost murdered her. He did follow through with his promise after having her arrested on the stalking charge she had threatened me with all those years ago. She no longer worked as a publicist. Trent had made sure to spread the truth of her meddling far and wide, and she could no longer find anyone willing to hire her again. I couldn't find it in myself to care after everything we had been through.

"Momma! Did you see that?" T.J. bounced in his seat, the excitement coming off him in waves as Angelica clapped her gloved hands from my other side. "Daddy scored a goal!"

The entire hockey arena had just sat back down after stomping and cheering for my husband. I grinned at our little boy. He wanted to be a hockey player just like his dad. He and Trent had already spent more time out on the ice than I could count, learning how to skate, and already had a tiny hockey stick, perfect for his size. Angelica enjoyed gliding around the edges of the rink in her sparkling pink skates.

I rubbed my huge baby bump as I grinned out at the game, my eyes only on one player. "I saw, baby."

"I'm going to win goals, too, one day," he announced. "I'm going to be the bestest, just like my daddy."

I looked over at Trent Junior and couldn't resist running my hand over his thick, dark hair. "I know you will, honey. And Daddy and I will watch you win every one of them."

I looked back up, looking for my husband's number, finding him easily. He looked at me, his grin easy to see. He pointed his stick at me, mouthing the words, "I love you." I placed my hand over my heart as it flipped in my chest. "I love you, too." He couldn't hear the words, but I knew he felt them as he read them on my lips.

We'd had an amazing beginning and a heartbreaking middle, but our story was turning out to be the most beautiful adventure, and I couldn't wait to see what else was in store for us.

ABOUT THE AUTHOR

R. Sullins is a USA Today bestselling author, an International Bestseller, and a KDP All Star.

Family is number one in her life, followed by her menagerie of pets. Be patient with her, she's not very good at peopling.

She is a lover of fairies, tattoos, and coffee cups, has a vast collection of them all, and receives a glare from her teenager every time she brings home a new cup to squeeze into the cabinet.

When she's not writing, you will probably be able to find her reading a book. But, no matter what genre you find her immersed in, there is always one thing that her favorite stories have in common...you will never, ever find her reading any book with cheating. So rest assured! She will never write one, either.

A bit of drama, a dash of spice, a little bit of innocence, and a large dab of alpha is what makes up the recipe for her stories. Find more of her here: www.rsullins.com

FREE BOOK

For a **FREE SHORT STORY** THAT IS ONLY AVAILABLE THROUGH THIS LINK - JOIN MY NEWSLETTER!

She wasn't sure what she was doing at the cabin.

It was run down and needed serious attention.

She should sell it and be done with it, but her grandmother left it to her.

It was all she had left in the world.

He hadn't shifted back into his human form for years.

He held the responsibility for his family's death in his heart.

The only thing that kept him moving one paw in front of the other

was the need to make sure the same fate didn't happen to anyone else in his pack.

Then everything changed when a new scent filled the forest.

How was the Alpha wolf supposed to stay away when her scent just kept drawing him in?

TEMPTING THE WOLF BY R SULLINS

ALSO BY R SULLINS

CONTEMPORARY ROMANCE

Cry For Me - All For You series Book 1

A high school romance

Light from the Dark - Protecting What's Theirs

An MMF serial killer romance

The Nightmare King - Book One in The Nightmare Duet

An MC romance

The Queen of Nightmares - Book Two in The Nightmare Duet

An MC romance

Planned releases:

Break For Me

An All For You novel

Fall For Me

An All For You novel

Running Home

A contemporary romance

PARANORMAL ROMANCE

Lovely Darkness - A Demons Within book

A standalone demon romance in an ongoing story arc

Craving Darkness - A Demons Within book

A standalone demon romance in an ongoing story arc

The Hunter series

Hunter's Blood is book one in a <u>complete</u> vampire trilogy

Jared

A standalone in the Hunter series

Those Who Whisper

A standalone ghost romance

Planned releases:

<u>Crimson Fate</u>

A standalone in The Hunter series

<u>Ohhs, Ahhhs, and Orbs</u>

A witchy murder mystery romance

SPICY & SWEET INSTA LOVE SHORTS

Standalone short stories

Igniting Ember

A firefighter romance

Her Temporary Boss

A boss/CEO romance

The Worst Witch

A witchy romance

Soothing Santa

A holiday romance

<u>Fragile Hearts</u>

A holiday romance

Printed in Great Britain
by Amazon